W. SOMERSET MAUGHAM

Appointment

ADAPTED BY ALAN BENJAMIN
ILLUSTRATED BY

Roger Essley

GREEN TIGER PRESS
Published by Simon & Schuster
New York · London · Toronto · Sydney · Tokyo · Singapore

*Centuries ago, in the city of Baghdad, lived a
wealthy merchant with his servant, Abdullah.*

Please lend me your horse so that I may ride to Samarra
and escape whatever fate she has in mind for me."

*The merchant, who loved his servant well, helped him mount
his horse, and watched him ride off toward Samarra.*

*Afraid for Abdullah, the merchant went himself to
the marketplace to seek out the old woman.*

*When she stepped out of the fortuneteller's tent,
he recognized her at once.*

"Why," he asked her, "did you stare so threateningly
at my good servant, Abdullah, this morning?"

For Ellen O'Hara—A.B.

To my mother, Betsy,
and my father, Harry—R.E.

GREEN TIGER PRESS
Simon & Schuster Building
Rockefeller Center
1230 Avenue of the Americas
New York, New York 10020
Text copyright © 1993 by Simon & Schuster.
Illustration copyright © 1993 by Roger Essley.
All rights reserved including the right of
reproduction in whole or in part in any form.
GREEN TIGER PRESS is an imprint of Simon & Schuster.
Designed by Alan Benjamin
Manufactured in the United States of America
10 9 8 7 6 5 4 3 2 1

Library of Congress Cataloging-in-Publication Data
Benjamin, Alan. Appointment/adapted by Alan Benjamin;
illustrated by Roger Essley. p. cm. "Based on Appointment
in Samarra, from Sheppy, by W.S. Maugham"—T.p. verso.
Summary: Death, disguised as an old woman, searches for
Abdullah the servant. [1. Death—fiction. 2. Household
employees—Fiction. 3. Baghdad (Iraq)—Fiction.]
I. Essley, Roger, ill. II. Title. PZ7.B4346Ap 1993
[Fic]—dc20 92-391 CIP ISBN 0-671-75887-X

Based on Appointment in Samarra *from* Sheppy
by W.S. Maugham. Copyright 1933 by W. S. Maugham.
Used by permission of Doubleday, a division of
Bantam Doubleday Dell Publishing Group, Inc.